MW01233521

My Home Country

GUATEMALA

IS MY HOME

For a free color catalog describing Gareth Stevens' list of high-quality books, call 1-800-341-3569 (USA) or 1-800-461-9120 (Canada).

For their help in the preparation of *Guatemala Is My Home,* the editors gratefully thank: Patricia Mendoza, First Secretary, Embassy of Guatemala, Washington, DC; Professor Rosa Helena Chinchilla, University of Wisconsin-Milwaukee; Professor Michael Fleet, Marquette University, Milwaukee; and Professor Howard Handelman, University of Wisconsin-Milwaukee.

Flag illustration on page 42, © Flag Research Center

Library of Congress Cataloging-in-Publication Data

Lantier-Sampon, Patricia.
    Guatemala is my home / adapted from Ronnie Cummins' Children of the world, Guatemala, by Patricia Lantier-Sampon ; photographs by Rose Welch.
       p. cm. — (My home country)
    Includes bibliographical references and index.
    Summary: A look at the life of a twelve-year-old Mayan Indian girl and her family living in the lakeside village of Santiago Atitlán. Includes a section with information on Guatemala.
    ISBN 0-8368-0901-7
    1. Guatemala—Social life and customs—Juvenile literature. [1. Family life—Guatemala. 2. Guatemala.] I. Welch, Rose, ill. II. Cummins, Ronnie. Guatemala. III. Title. IV. Series.
F1463.5.L36 1993
972.81—dc20
                                                         92-34675

Edited, designed, and produced by

Gareth Stevens Publishing
1555 North RiverCenter Drive, Suite 201
Milwaukee, Wisconsin 53212, USA

Text, photographs, and format © 1993 by Gareth Stevens, Inc. First published in the United States and Canada in 1992 by Gareth Stevens, Inc. This U.S. edition is abridged from *Children of the World: Guatemala,* © 1990 by Gareth Stevens, Inc., with text by Ronnie Cummins and photographs by Rose Welch.

Series editors: Barbara Behm and Beth Karpfinger
Cover design: Kristi Ludwig
Layout: Kate Kriege
Map design: Sheri Gibbs

Printed in the United States of America

1 2 3 4 5 6 7 8 9 97 96 95 94 93

My Home Country

GUATEMALA

IS MY HOME

Adapted from Ronnie Cummins'
Children of the World: Guatemala

by Patricia Lantier-Sampon
Photographs by Rose Welch

Gareth Stevens Publishing
MILWAUKEE

Twelve-year-old Maria belongs to a Mayan Indian tribe called the Tzutuhils. She lives in the town of Santiago Atitlán. Maria is in the fourth grade and would like to become a schoolteacher. She works hard at school and at home but always finds time to play.

To enhance this book's value in libraries and classrooms, clear and simple reference sections include up-to-date information about Guatemala's history, land and climate, people and language, education, and religion. *Guatemala Is My Home* also features a large and colorful map, bibliography, glossary, simple index, research topics, and activity projects designed especially for young readers.

The living conditions and experiences of children in Guatemala vary according to economic, environmental, and ethnic circumstances. The reference sections help bring to life for young readers the diversity and richness of the culture and heritage of Guatemala. Of particular interest are discussions of the traditional ways of the Mayan Indians from the Spanish Conquest to modern times.

My Home Country includes the following titles:

Canada	*Nicaragua*
Costa Rica	*Peru*
Cuba	*Poland*
El Salvador	*South Africa*
Guatemala	*Vietnam*
Ireland	*Zambia*

CONTENTS

Maria Reanda stands with her family behind their Santiago Atitlán home.

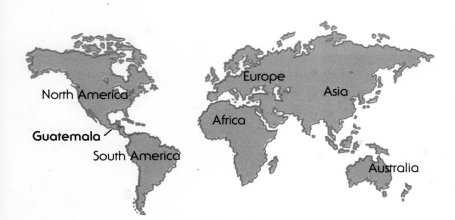

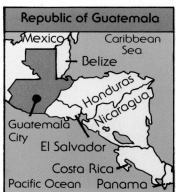

LIVING IN GUATEMALA:
Maria, a Girl from Lake Atitlán

Twelve-year-old Maria de los Angeles Reanda belongs to a Mayan Indian tribe called the Tzutuhil. She lives with her parents and her older brother, Pedro, in the Guatemalan town of Santiago Atitlán. Santiago Atitlán lies on the southwestern shore of Lake Atitlán. The town sits at the base of three large volcanoes.

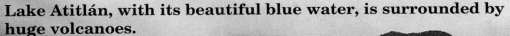

Lake Atitlán, with its beautiful blue water, is surrounded by huge volcanoes.

The San Pedro volcano rises in the background of Santiago Atitlán.

The simple Reanda house stands on a hill.

At Home on the Lake

Maria loves to hear stories and legends about Guatemala. One legend explains how Lake Atitlán came to be: Jesus' apostles once passed through Guatemala. Tired and thirsty, they stopped to rest. "How sad it is that there is no water here," said Saint James. He then dug a hole in the ground and threw in the drinking water that was left over from their lunch. The pool of water grew until it became beautiful Lake Atitlán.

◀ Maria proudly shows off Canela, her new puppy.

11

Maria loves her family's one-room house with the walled-in backyard. Her mother's family built it more than 100 years ago.

Only a few houses in Santiago Atitlán have indoor plumbing or electricity. For drinking and cooking, Maria and her family carry water from the lake, where they also bathe. Maria's house has one light bulb in the kitchen.

Maria fills a water jug at the lake. ▶
Below: A back view of the Reanda house.

Early Mornings

The Reandas' day starts at 4:30 a.m. Maria and her mother prepare breakfast. Pedro and Maria's father, Diego, collect firewood, fish in the lake, or gather food from the garden.

Maria lights a fire to heat their breakfast of black beans, tortillas, and coffee. Then she carries a bowl of corn to the village *molino,* or corn grinder. The molino grinds the corn into a paste used to make tortillas.

Top: Before sunrise, women and girls from the village bring corn to the molino.
Bottom: The sun has not risen yet as Maria returns to the house with a bowl of ground corn paste, called *masa.*

14

Top: Maria's mother shows her how to knead dough.
Left: Diego's recorder music fills the early-morning stillness.
Above: Maria offers a tiny bit of her breakfast to one of the rabbits in the backyard.

A Short School Day

Maria is in the fourth grade at Mateo Herrera Elementary School. The school year begins in January and ends in October, and classes last four hours each day.

Maria studies hard because someday she wants to be a schoolteacher. Today, she is eager to finish her math, reading, writing, and science classes so she can go to art, which is her favorite class.

Sometimes, it is hard for Maria to concentrate in class.

Above: Maria's class lines up in front of school. Mateo Herrera Elementary is small, simple, and crowded.
Left: Maria's classmate looks up from his schoolwork.

Above insets and background: Recess is a time for wild play and talking with friends.

18

Maria enjoys playing with her schoolmates. Her favorite sport is basketball, and she and her friends play almost every day. Pedro and his friends spend most of their time playing soccer.

When classes begin, the teacher often has a lesson on the board for the children to copy. Because the government of Guatemala gives so little money for education, Maria's school cannot afford many textbooks.

Above inset: Maria's school supplies are spread out beside the book bag that Pedro embroidered for her.

Above: Diego and Maria share an interest in books and learning. Left: A group of boys crowd around the snack table, each trying to wiggle his way to the front.

Many people in Santiago Atitlán cannot go to school because they must work to support their families. Diego learned to read and write on his own, but he wants a better education for his children. He wants Maria and Pedro to study hard.

Maria and Pedro hope to attend high school. But this means they will have to live away from home. The Reandas are saving money so Pedro can go to high school next year.

Maria's mother stirs a big bowl of tomato sauce.

No Time to Waste

Maria and Pedro help with chores before and after school. While Diego and Pedro work in the fields and fish on the lake, Maria and her mother work at home.

Maria and her mother shape tortillas, grind tomato paste, scrub clothing at the lake, and weave colorful cloth. Maria's favorite chore is feeding the rabbits and chickens.

Right: Maria's mother prepares a meal of tomato sauce wrapped in banana-tree leaves.
Below and bottom: Banana-tree leaves are also fed to animals.

Maria tries to have fun while she works. Even hauling water and washing clothes can be fun, since these chores give Maria time to visit with her friends. The girls talk while carrying water from the lake in jugs that they balance on their heads. They have to make this trip many times each day.

Maria and her mother work hard to keep the family's clothes clean. They must make many trips to the lake to wash the clothes by hand. After soaping the clothes, Maria uses a rock as a washboard. She then spreads the clean clothes in the sun to dry.

◀ Maria scrubs the family wash against a huge rock.
Below: Maria and a friend play a game of marbles. When the game is finished, the girls fill the water jugs.

Canoes, called *cayucos*, are moored along the lakeshore. Maria's family has a canoe that looks like one of these.

Diego and Pedro farm and fish to provide food for the family. On some days, they spend many hours fishing on Lake Atitlán. On other days, they farm their own land or help farm their relatives' fields.

The Reandas grow corn, beans, squash, tomatoes, cucumbers, and peppers. They also have orange trees and coffee trees.

Top: Diego and Pedro weave
reeds to make a mat. When
they are through weaving the
mats, they dry them in the
sun. The dried mats will be
used for sleeping.
Above: A close-up of the mat
shows its weaving pattern.
Right: Diego picks ripe
coffee beans.

Above: A small boy works on a sugarcane plantation.

◄ Diego and Pedro pick black beans from the garden. This land has been in the Reanda family for generations.

During the rainy season, from May through October, the garden gets plenty of water. But during the dry months, Diego and Pedro must carry water from the lake to irrigate their plants. Sometimes, Maria helps her father and brother in the fields.

Many villagers do not have enough land to feed their families, so they must buy some of their food. They earn extra money by working on nearby coffee, sugarcane, and cotton plantations.

29

Top: The orphanage has a thatched roof that is common to many Guatemalan buildings.
Above: These girls work for the orphanage.
Above: A young orphan looks shyly at the camera.

Time Out for Maria

Although Maria works hard, she still finds time to have fun. After finishing her homework each day, she visits her friends Candelaria and Elena. Often, the girls walk to the lake, stopping to talk with the small children at the nearby orphanage.

Maria and Pedro do many things together. They play with Maria's puppy, Canela, or ride in the canoe. Their favorite pastime is making colorful paintings of Guatemalan landscapes, which they later sell to tourists.

Pedro takes Maria for a ride in the family canoe.

One of Pedro's watercolors shows the temple of Maximón.

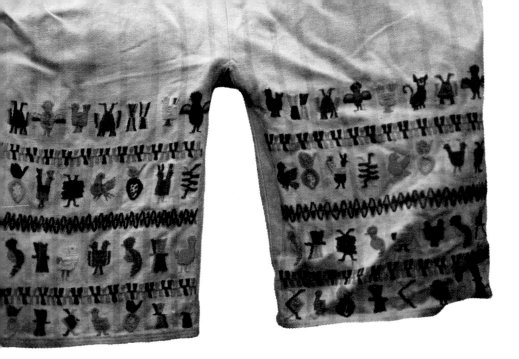

Maria's mother has sewn colorful designs on this pair of shorts.

An Ancient Art

Weaving is an important skill in Guatemala. Using a simple loom, Maria's mother creates nearly everything the family wears. She is now teaching Maria to weave.

Maria enjoys selling the family's handicraft to tourists. Tourists come from all over the world and are always eager to buy her mother's weavings or the watercolors she and Pedro create.

Lake Atitlán's Colorful Markets

The family sells most of its produce and art-work at the market of Santiago Atitlán. Maria and her mother go to the market almost every day. Like her mother, Maria carries her produce in a basket balanced on her head.

Maria and Pedro use a scale to weigh the beans they will sell in the market.

The market offers everything from fresh meat and fish to vegetables and grains. Clothing, gardening tools, canned goods, and household supplies are also available.

Top: This woman sells pottery and takes care of her children at the same time.
Right: A young Indian woman shows off the colorful dress of her people.

Maria, Pedro, Diego — and Canela — travel across Lake Atitlán to gather firewood.

A Canoe Trip across the Lake

The Reanda family often travels by canoe. Today, Maria, Diego, and Pedro are going across the lake to collect firewood. Maria can't wait to go because her father has said she can paddle the canoe part of the way.

Above left: Maria carries a huge bundle of firewood.
Above right: If Canela had known that a bath was part of the trip, she probably wouldn't have come along.

They pull the canoe to shore near the San Pedro volcano. Then they walk along mountain paths, gathering branches and sticks. Maria and Pedro try to see who can balance the largest bundle of firewood.

Visiting the Temple of Maximón

Today, the Reanda family visits the temple of Maximón, traditional god of the Tzutuhil people. Because the season for planting is near, the Reandas will ask Maximón to bless the coming crops. As many Tzutuhils do, Maria and her family honor both the God of Christianity and Maximón, the Mayan God.

The villagers decorate the statue of Maximón with colorful scarves.

◀ Maria, Diego, and Pedro pose with a statue of Maximón.

Guatemalans celebrate Good Friday with a huge procession that winds through the street.

A Week of Celebration

Semana Santa, or Holy Week, is the year's biggest religious festival. Thousands of villagers come to town for the festival, which starts on Palm Sunday, the Sunday before Easter, and continues for seven days. Maria's family goes to Mass, marches in processions, and visits friends and relatives. Schools close at this time, and most people stop working.

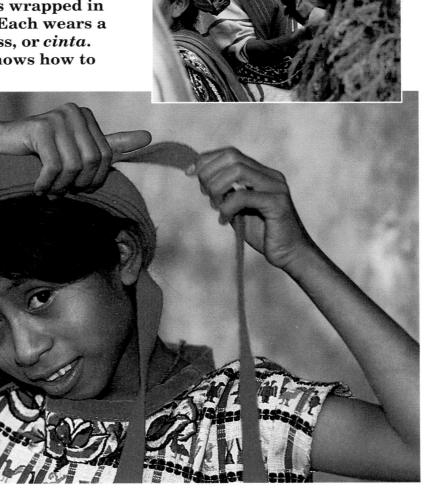

Right: The women of Santiago Atitlán join the procession, carrying candles wrapped in banana leaves. Each wears a special headdress, or *cinta*. **Below:** Maria shows how to make a cinta.

MORE FACTS ABOUT: Guatemala

Official Name: República de Guatemala
(ray-POO-blee-kah deh wha-teh-MAH-lah)
Republic of Guatemala

Capital: Guatemala City

History

The Mayan Indians were the first people to live in
what is now Guatemala. Between 2500 BC and AD
1000, these Indians built a complex civilization
and remained in power until the Spanish
conquistadors enslaved them in 1523. In 1821,
Guatemala declared independence from Spain, but
the tiny country's early years of independence were
troubled.   A revolution in 1871 brought Justo
Rufino Barrios to power. Barrios encouraged the
country's economic development, but the situation
for the Indians and the poor stayed much the same
as it had under the Spaniards. In 1944, elections
were held and for the first time in Guatemala's
history, all citizens enjoyed equal rights. In 1954, a
military dictatorship took power. Since that time,
political violence has raged in Guatemala, with the
military on one side and rebel groups on the other.
In 1986, the people elected a civilian government
headed by Vinicio Cerezo Arévalo, but peace and

change still have not come to the country.

Guatemala is a republic of 22 states. The head of government is the president, but for most of the 20th century, the army has ruled the country.

Land and Climate

Guatemala is the third largest country in Central America. It is bordered by the countries of Mexico, Belize, Honduras, and El Salvador. Guatemala has two basic types of land surfaces: lowlands and central mountain highlands. The highlands are dotted with volcanoes, some of which are active. Guatemala has a wide range of climates.

People and Language

After the arrival of the Spaniards, Guatemalans gradually became a people of both Spanish and Indian blood. By 1989, Guatemala's population was about 9,000,000. Spanish has long been the

The basic unit of money in Guatemala is the *quetzal*.

official language of Guatemala, but over 20 Mayan languages are still spoken.

Education

Guatemalan children between the ages of 7 and 14 years must attend school. But many children must also work to help support their families. As a result, most children do not complete elementary school, and only 10% attend high school or college. Over half of Guatemala's people cannot read or write.

Religion

Many Guatemalans attend church services regularly, and over 80% of the people belong to the Roman Catholic church. The Indians usually practice a mixture of Catholic and Mayan beliefs.

Sports and Recreation

The most popular sport in Guatemala is soccer. Guatemalans also enjoy basketball, baseball, swimming, biking, and running.

Guatemalans in North America

Because of Guatemala's political problems, hundreds of thousands of Guatemalans have fled the country. Several hundred thousand are living in Mexico, and several hundred thousand more are living in the United States and Canada.

Glossary of Useful Guatemalan (Spanish) Terms

cayucos (kah-YOU-kohs): canoes.

cinta (SEEN-tah): a headdress.

Maximón (mah-she-MOHN): traditional god of the Tzutuhils.

molino (moe-LEE-noh): corn grinder.

tortilla (tor-TEE-yah): a round cake of cornmeal or wheat flour, often filled with meat or cheese.

More Books about Guatemala

Guatemala, a Country Study. Nyrop, editor (US Government Printing Office)
Guatemala in Pictures. Lerner Publications Dept. of Geography Staff (Lerner)
Hello Guatemala. Karen (Grosset & Dunlap)

Things to Do

1. For a pen pal, write to: Worldwide Pen Friends, P.O. Box 39097, Downey, CA 90241. Be sure to tell them what country you want your pen pal to be from. Also include your full name, age, and address.

2. The quetzal is also Guatemala's national bird. Find out more about this rare bird and what it looks like.

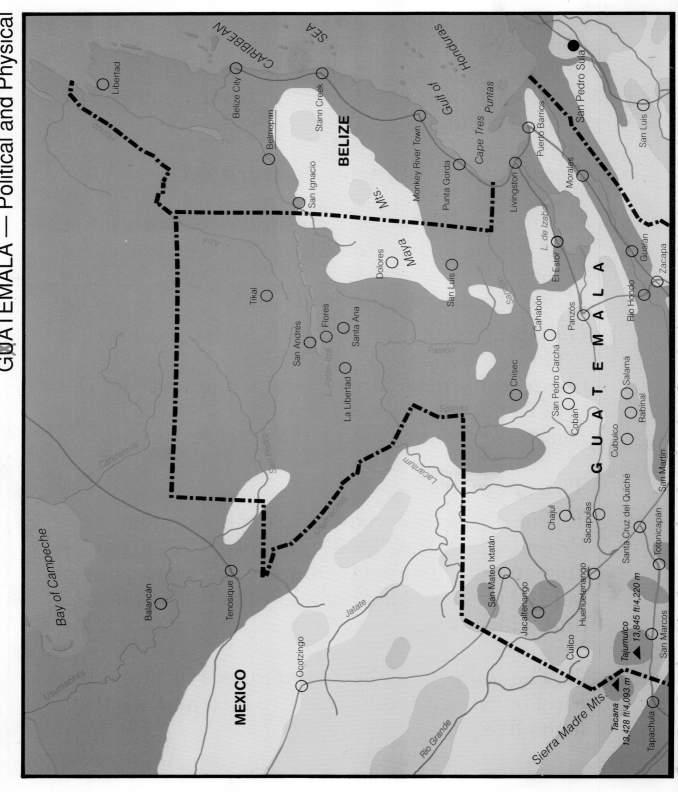

GUATEMALA — Political and Physical

MEXICO

BELIZE

GUATEMALA

CARIBBEAN SEA

Gulf of Honduras

Bay of Campeche

Libertad

Belize City

Belmopan

Stann Creek

San Ignacio

Monkey River Town

Punta Gorda

Cape Tres Puntas

San Pedro Sula

San Luis

Puerto Barrios

Morales

Livingston

L. de Izabal

El Estor

Guatán

Zacapa

Río Hondo

Dolores

San Luis

Maya Mts.

Cahabón

Panzós

San Pedro Carchá

Salamá

Rabinal

Chisec

Cobán

Cubulco

San Martín

Tikal

San Andrés

Flores

L. Petén-Itzá

Santa Ana

La Libertad

Salinas

Chajul

Sacapulas

Santa Cruz del Quiché

Totonicapán

San Mateo Ixtatán

Jacaltenango

Huehuetenango

Cuilco

San Marcos

▲ Tajumulco 13,845 ft/4,220 m

▲ Tacana 13,428 ft/4,093 m

Tapachula

Ocotzingo

Tenosique

Balancán

Sierra Madre Mts.

Hondo

Azul

Candelaria

San Pedro

Pasión

Sarstún

Lacantún

Usumacinta

Jatate

Rio Grande

Usumacinta

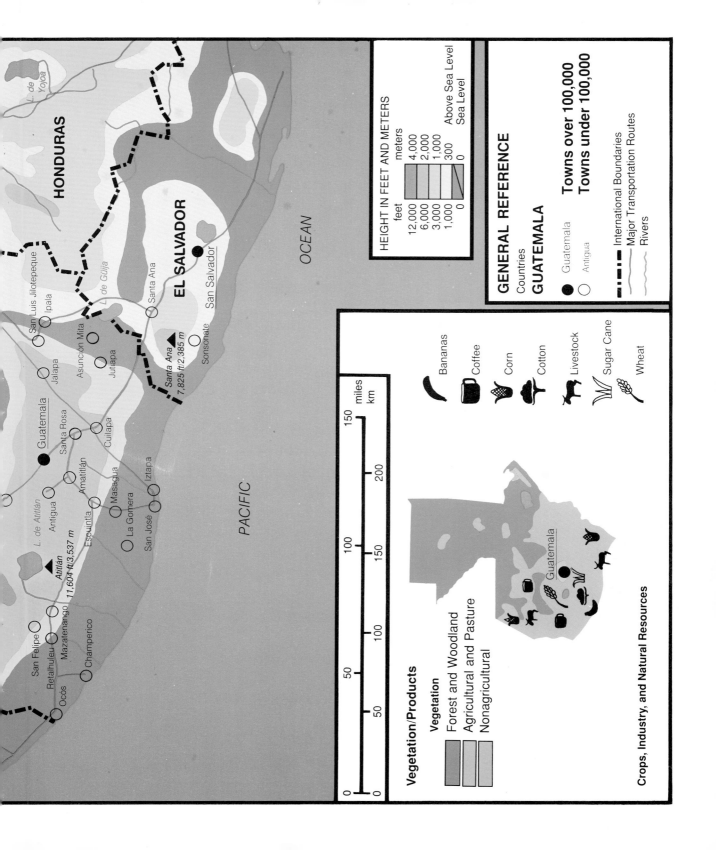

Index